Tins, Trolls and

VALIANT VIKINGS

D1439480

Written by
Shalini Vallepur

Illustrated by
Amy Li

©2022 BookLife Publishing Ltd.
King's Lynn, Norfolk, PE30 4LS, UK

ISBN 978-1-80155-460-2

Tins, Trolls and Valiant Vikings
Written by Shalini Vallepur
Edited by Madeline Tyler
Illustrated by Amy Li

Meet the
CHARACTERS

Mr Meridell

Riya

Emma

Chapter One

Lots of Lentils

"All food donations to the hall!" Mr Meridell called, just as the school day was beginning.

It was harvest festival at Greenlake Primary School and all the students had brought in food to donate to charity. Riya's bag was bursting with all sorts of tins. She dragged it towards the hall when,

just like that, the bag split!
She bent down to pick up the
rolling tins when she heard
laughter.

"Not now, Emma,"

Riya groaned.

"Ha ha! You dropped everything!" Emma laughed, picking up a tin. "Lentils? What are lentils?"

"Get off it!" yelled Riya.

"Sounds horrible. Besides, everyone will want some of my beans!" Emma held a shiny tin in Riya's face. "Everyone likes beans on toast, not lentils on toast. My beans are sure to win!"

Riya glared at Emma as she carried her tins to the hall. There were piles of tins and boxes full of food. "There's no winner, Emma," Riya said.

"There is. The best things get made into a dish this afternoon," Emma sneered. "And we all know it won't be yours." Riya could have growled, but Mr Meridell appeared.

"Hurry along you two, it's time for class," he said with a smile. "And no running!" Riya and Emma stared at each other as they left the hall. As soon as they were out of Mr Meridell's sight, they raced to their classroom.

Chapter Two

Mr Meridell's
Marvelous Lesson

"As you all know, today is harvest festival. We celebrate it here at Greenlake Primary by collecting food and cooking up meals to give to a local shelter. But let's look at how people have celebrated harvest festivals in history," Mr Meridell said. "Lots of harvest festivals mark the start of winter, when it's too cold to grow any food. The Vikings had a festival called Winter Nights."

Emma poked Riya in the back. "I bet the Vikings didn't eat lentils," she whispered. Riya ignored her.

"Some groups believed that after Winter Nights, ghosts and trolls roamed the roads," Mr Meridell said.

He held up a picture of a troll. It had long shaggy hair, big feet with long toenails and a large nose. Some of the class started to laugh.

"Laugh all you like, but you wouldn't want to meet a troll. They searched the lands for food. Of course, they didn't find any because it had all been harvested..."

Riya put her hand up.

"So, what did the trolls eat?" Riya gulped.

"Some say they ate twigs, others say they feasted on children," Mr Meridell said as the class gasped. "But others say that they were not real and just a scary story." Riya didn't know what to believe. Emma poked her back again.

"The trolls will come
for you!" she giggled.

"The trolls will come after
you and your
stinky, farty
beans," Riya
snapped
at Emma.
The entire
class turned
around and

Mr Meridell put his hands on his hips.

"Sorry..." Riya said.

Mr Meridell set them work to do and everyone sat at their tables. They had been set a harvest project. They had to make a poster that showed a Viking feast. Riya sat in silence and sketched out a big troll at a dinner table while

everybody else in the class chatted and joked around. Mr Meridell came over and looked at Riya's drawing.

"You're a bit quiet today, are you OK?" he said.

"I want to get my troll drawing just right," Riya said.

"There's a book in the library called 'Valiant Vikings'. It has loads of drawings of

Viking villages and even some trolls. In fact, it can help you get a closer look at some trolls..." Mr Meridell said. Riya beamed; she would check it out at lunchtime. Mr Meridell stood up to speak to the class.

"It's time for lunch! Don't forget, we will be cooking with the donated food this afternoon!" Mr Meridell

called as everybody dashed
for lunch.

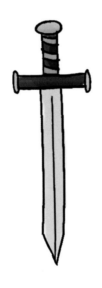

Chapter Three

Going Down the Gateway

Riya made her way to the library and she thought about Emma's jabs in the morning. Who hadn't heard of lentils? Riya ate them all the time! She took her lunchbox and headed towards the library to look for the book that Mr Meridell suggested.

"I wonder what the Vikings ate...?" she thought

as she munched on her sandwich. She stood on her tiptoes and searched for 'Valiant Vikings' on the shelves. When she found it, she slid the book out and took a step back. But her foot never touched the ground. She yelped and fell backwards.

"Ahhhh!" Riya closed her eyes and cried out.

Her stomach jolted as she fell backwards. Down, down, down, she kept falling. The air whooshed in her ears and hair flew around her. She opened her eyes but all she could see was flashing colours, swirls of light and for some reason, Mr Meridell's eyes.

"Help!" she cried. She landed on her bum with

a hard thud. "Ouch!" She looked around.

'Where am I? What's going on?' she thought. She was in a field and she could see a dirt road nearby. It was daytime at school, but here it was dusk. She took a deep breath and started to stand up when a boy about her age jumped in front of her.

"Argh! Die troll!" he yelled. Riya screamed and the boy stopped. "Oh, you're not a troll," the boy said as he turned away. Riya looked down at herself. She wasn't wearing her school uniform anymore. She was wearing a simple cloth dress and brown leather shoes. She turned her head and it hurt a little – her hair was in tight plaits. When did this happen? She started to panic, then she noticed a book by her side. The Valiant

Vikings book had somehow stayed with her. When she looked back up, she saw a Viking village over the hills and she gasped.

Chapter Four

The Valiant Viking Village

Riya squinted her eyes to
see the Viking village in the
distance. She could see
dancing and hear the sound of
music, which was carried up
the hill by the wind. She didn't
know what to do except stare
blankly ahead of her. Was
this to do with the Valiant
Viking book? She pinched
her arm and felt it – it was not

a dream.

"If you're here to make fun of me, then you can go away," a voice said. It was the boy. He was sitting on a nearby rock looking gloomy. Riya couldn't speak. "You can tell them that I screamed, I don't care anymore."

"What's going on?" Riya finally said. The boy turned

around to look at her.

"I'm protecting the village from trolls," he said. "Pete, Bog and Harald are supposed to be here too, but they ran off to steal food from the feast.

If a troll shows up, then I will beat him and show everyone that I'm the bravest!"

Trolls? Feast? A valiant Viking village? It suddenly clicked. Riya had fallen down the strange gateway and landed in a Viking harvest festival. It was Winter Nights!

"Beating a troll? How will you do that?" Riya squeaked.

"The sword of course," said the boy. He pointed to a large sword that stuck in the ground. "Although, Harald put it there and I can't get it out..." he trailed off. "Look, you should go back to the village. It's not safe out here without a weapon of your own."

"But I don't know where I

am," Riya answered. The boy narrowed his eyes.

"You're not from here, are you?" he said. He suddenly jumped on the rock and pressed his hand to his chest. "My name is Benethor Bravefoot, and I swear to protect you from the trolls that curse our land on this very night!"

"My name is Riya, um, Riya Righthanded," she said. She hid the Valiant Vikings book behind her back. How could she explain where the book came from?

"Come, Riya Righthanded! I shall lead you home this instant!" Benethor swooped down and grabbed her hand. He led her to a dirt road and

immediately crouched down.
"Stay low! I hear something,"
he whispered.
Coming up
the little
dirt road
were three
monstrous
trolls...

Chapter Five

The Three Trolls

The trolls stomped their way down the road. Dust and dirt flew into the air with every step. They made odd grunting noises. One was scratching its bottom. At first, Riya was terrified, but then the smell hit her. She covered her nose with her hand and groaned. She had never smelled anything so bad

in her life.

"I feel sick!" Riya said in a croaky whisper. It was a rotten funk of spoiled eggs, mouldy cheese and what could only be described as poo.

"This way," Benethor said – he was a boy on a mission. He skilfully rolled on the ground away from the trolls and crouched behind a tree.

Riya scurried after. She clutched the Valiant Vikings book close to her chest.

"Put that down, we need to fight," hissed Benethor.

"Fight? But I don't know how to fight!" Riya cried.

"Not so loud! This is my chance to prove how brave I am," Benethor said. "But first, you have to help me pull the

sword out of the ground.
I can't do it on my own."

They were about to move back to the sword when the ground shook. They looked up with worry. One of the trolls had tripped over.

"OWWWWWW!"

the troll roared. Riya jumped out of her skin and dropped Valiant Vikings.

Benethor covered his ears. **"MY KNEEEEEE!"** Riya poked her head around the tree and saw that the troll had started to sob. Big fat tears rolled down its cheeks and

off its large nose.

"Get up!" one of the other trolls said in a gruff voice.

"I can't!" bawled the fallen troll. "I'm too hungry! I can't move!"

The two standing trolls shrugged, and instead of helping it up, they both plonked their bottoms in the middle of the road.

"I'm hungry too," one of them sighed. "The fields are empty. The fruits are gone. We've had nothing to eat for three days!" The fallen troll sobbed even louder.

"I just want some beautiful, boiled cabbage! I'm bored of eating stinky, slimy mud pies!" the fallen troll cried and cried.

"Look, there's nobody here protecting the village. We can make a run for it and steal some food from the feast," one said. Riya saw Benethor freeze beside her.

"Let's go get the sword, we have to protect the village," Riya hissed. Benethor shook his head and pointed down the dirt road. Coming up the path, with their hands full of stolen food, were Pete, Bog and Harald.

Chapter Six

Pete, Bog and Hungry Harald

Pete, Bog and Harald froze. Harald dropped the apples he was carrying, and they rolled down the road towards the trolls.

"Food!" the trolls yelled.

"T—trolls!" the boys yelled.

Two of the trolls stood up on shaky legs. The boys' legs were shaking too, and they were too scared to run away.

"Where's Benethor? He's meant to be protecting the village!" Pete shouted.

"Trolls! Trolls! They're going to eat us alive!" Harald cried. The fallen troll was still on the floor, wailing.

"Get up, now's our chance! They've got food!" the two trolls tried to get the fallen troll to stand up, but it would

not budge.

"I don't want to fight! I just want to eat!" the fallen troll said.

"Quick, let's get the sword!" Riya said from behind the tree, but Benethor did not move. He looked extremely confused.

"I don't understand. Look at that troll, it won't stop

crying. Pete, Bog and Harald are too scared to fight, they're just standing there," said Benethor. Riya realised that the trolls were not as scary as they once thought.

"Benethor, the trolls don't want to eat children, they want to eat cabbage! You need to convince Pete, Bog and Harald to share their food,"

Riya said. They watched as
the three stinky trolls and the
three greedy boys argued.

"Look here you stinking
trolls! This bread is the only
bread I like, and I will NOT
be eaten by you before I get
to enjoy it!" Pete bellowed.

"Nobody cares, maggot!
Hand over the loaf and we will
go away!" a troll argued back.

"We just need a nibble–"

"Never! These are our
nibbles! We are hungry
warriors, and we will never
give our food to something

as stinky as you!" Harald
yelled.

Two of the trolls roared
in anger. They were about
to charge. Riya grabbed
Benethor's hand, leapt out
from behind the tree and
stood between the stinky
trolls and the greedy boys.

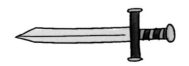

Chapter Seven

Riya Righthanded
to the Rescue

"Enough!" Riya shouted. Everybody froze. "You're all being silly! Nobody wants to fight, the trolls just want food, like the rest of us!"

"Benethor! You're alive!" said Bog, ignoring Riya. "Quick, beat those trolls!"

"Who are you?" Pete said to Riya. Although he

was shaking at the sight of the trolls, Benethor stepped forward.

"This is Riya Righthanded, and everything she's saying is true! We must not fight. Don't you see? Every year we harvest the fields. We have a big feast and there's so much food to go around, but we leave nothing for the trolls!" Benethor said.

The fallen troll sniffled.

   "Pete, tear that bread in
half. Harald, you don't need
ten apples all to yourself!
And Bog, what were you going

to do with those cabbages anyway?" Bog shrugged. The trolls looked at Benethor with wonder.

"Do you mean it, little maggot?" the fallen troll whimpered in delight. Benethor nodded.

"Fine," Pete said. "If it means you will go away." He tore the loaf of bread in half

and stepped forward slowly.
He put the bread down on the
road. Bog and Harald did the
same with the cabbage and
apples. The fallen troll started
to cry again, but they were

happy tears this time.

"Thank you so much!" the fallen troll cried. "Finally, we have something to eat!"

"We will make sure to leave you some food during next year's harvest," said Benethor. "That way, you won't have to eat slimy mud pies."

"We won't forget this!"

the trolls said. They scooped
the food in their arms and
skipped away down the dirt
road. The boys crowded
around Benethor and patted
him on the back.

"Well done, Benethor!"

"You were so brave!"

"It wasn't just me,"
Benethor said, "Riya
Righthanded gave me

the idea–" Benethor turned to thank Riya, but she was gone.

Chapter Eight

Lentil Soup

Riya landed with a soft thud. She was back in the library. Her sandwich had fallen apart and made a mess on the carpet. Valiant Vikings lay on the floor. A voice suddenly snapped at her.

"What are you doing here? Lessons started five minutes ago!" the librarian said. Riya rubbed her bottom and made

her way back to her classroom.
What had happened? One
second she was watching the
trolls skipping with joy down
the road and the next second
she was falling through the
ground. Would she ever see
Benethor, Pete, Bog and
Harald again? Had she gone
back in time? Maybe she had
fallen asleep in the library and

it was all a dream.

"There you are, Riya," Mr Meridell said as she walked into the classroom. "Did you get a chance to read Valiant Vikings?"

"Yes, I did," Riya said. She sat down next to Emma.

"Did you get a closer look at some trolls?" Mr Meridell said, with a smile. Riya stared at him. Did Mr Meridell know what had happened?

"What did you do to your hair?" Emma asked. Riya's mouth fell open. Her hair was still tightly coiled in plaits. Mr Meridell started speaking.

"Now everybody is ready, it's time to cook a meal using the food donations! We have picked Riya's lentils and

Emma's beans! We will be
making a delicious lentil

and bean soup!" he said. Emma groaned.

"That's not fair! We can't have two winners!" Emma said.

"Let's not fight girls, it's not about winning," Mr Meridell said. "Harvest is about coming together and sharing food with those who may need it." Mr Meridell

turned to Riya and smiled
at her plaited hair. "Isn't that
right Riya?" Riya nodded,
she definitely agreed with
Mr Meridell.

Meet the author:
Shalini Vallepur

Passionate about books from a very young age, Shalini Vallepur received the award of Norfolk County Scholar for her outstanding grades. Later on she read English at the University of Leicester, where she stayed to complete her Modern Literature MA. Whilst at university, Shalini volunteered as a Storyteller to help children learn to read, which gave her experience and expertise in the way children pick up and retain information. She used her knowledge and her background and implemented them in the books that she has written for BookLife Publishing. Shalini's writing easily takes us to different worlds, and the serenity and quality of her words are sure to captivate any child who picks up her books.

Meet the illustrator:
Amy Li

Born in Derby, Amy has always wanted to become
a children's book illustrator, ever since falling in love
with the work of Nick Sharratt and Quentin Blake as
a child. She achieved a first class degree in Graphic
Design and Illustration at De Montfort University before
beginning her career at BookLife, during which time
she has designed and illustrated over 100 titles.
Amy's illustrations are always colourful, bright and
full of life, and bound to draw in any child who picks
up one of her books. Amy now resides in Norfolk,
where she lives with her partner and cat.